POPULAR CULTURE IN AMERICA

1800-1925

POPULAR CULTURE IN AMERICA

1800-1925

Advisory Editor
DAVID MANNING WHITE

Editorial Board
RAY B. BROWNE
MARSHALL W. FISHWICK
RUSSEL B. NYE

The
Stolen Pay Train

By
NICHOLAS CARTER
(*John R. Coryell*)

ARNO PRESS
A New York Times Company
New York • 1974

Reprint Edition 1974 by Arno Press Inc.

POPULAR CULTURE IN AMERICA: 1800-1925
ISBN for complete set: 0-405-06360-1
See last pages of this volume for titles.

Publisher's Note: This book was reprinted
from the best available copy.

Manufactured in the United States of America

————◆————

Library of Congress Cataloging in Publication Data

Coryell, John Russell, 1851-1924.
   The stolen pay train.

   (Popular culture in America)
   Reprint of the ed. published by Whitman Pub. Co.,
Racine, Wis.
   I. Title. II. Series.
PZ3.C82Sq20 [PS1449.C378]   813'.4   74-15733
ISBN 0-405-06368-7

The
Stolen Pay Train

By
NICHOLAS CARTER
(John R. Coryell)

Whitman Publishing Company
Racine, Wisconsin

Printed in U. S. A.

The Stolen Pay Train

CHAPTER I

"THIS IS SIMPLY IMPOSSIBLE!"

"A railroad train stolen? Well, this is interesting. Hello, Chick!"

"What's the matter, Nick?" asked the famous detective's assistant, stepping briskly into the study in response to the call of his chief.

"This gentleman is Morton Kane, president of the Chicago, Atchison and Denver Railroad," responded Nick, "and he has just handed me this telegram."

Chick took the telegram, which was in the cipher of the railroad company, with a translation written between the lines.

It contained this astonishing announcement:

"Monthly pay train missing. Left Denver at noon today. Arrived at Sumner 7:30. Cannot be traced beyond signal station at Haskins. Contained, besides our funds, heavy gold shipments from Park National and Morgan & Dix banks of Denver. Total loss over $1,000,-000. Must have been looted and destroyed. Engineer, fireman, and special guard of twelve men missing. No clew to method of the crime. Advise that you engage Nick Carter if possible, and have him come on at once. Wire when to expect him. No further details."

The railroad president glanced anxiously from one to the other, trying to read their faces and see how they accepted this startling piece of news.

"Well, gentlemen, what do you think of it? Of course this thing is simply impossible."

"Do you think the telegram is bogus?" asked Nick.

"It can't be."

"Why not?"

"Because it contains a secret sign from our representative in Sumner." He pointed out this sign.

Nick questioned him sharply in regard to this, and the character of the man who had sent the message.

"I believe that the telegram is genuine," said Nick, at last. "I don't think there's any doubt that, in some mysterious manner, that pay train has disappeared. On that theory, we will start West at once."

"Draw on us for all the money you may need," said Kane.

"All right. And now no time is to be lost. We will make the journey by airplane. Meanwhile you will keep yourself in constant communication with your representative out there, and notify us by wire of any important developments."

"I would like to go West with you," said Kane.

"You will do more good here, for you can receive reports from the West, and keep us posted. Now, good-by. We're off."

The journey westward was made with wonderful speed. Less than a day after that interview with the railroad president Nick and Chick arrived in Sumner.

It was early on an August morning. The plane had set them down on the outskirts of the town before sunrise, and had then turned back. All things had been arranged so that nobody in that region should guess that the two detectives had arrived.

Disguised as ranchmen, they made their way into the town. Then they separated. Nick went at once to find the representative of the railroad company. He found him at a desk in a private room in the rude station building.

The man was a wreck. He had scarcely slept since the train's loss. All that time he had been steadily at work on this mystery which baffled him at every turn.

He started up, and laid a hand upon a revolver when Nick entered the room suddenly and without warning.

"Don't shoot, Mr. Hampton," said the detective pleasantly. "It will make a noise, and that's what we don't want. I am Nick Carter, and I have come to have a quiet talk with you."

"Don't mind the gun," Hampton said. "The truth is, I'm so worn out and nervous that I'm not responsible for what I do."

"Tell me the story. I've only had a bare outline."

"You know about the pay train. It was made up of an engine and our regular pay car. It is strong as a safe; fireproof of course; and constructed especially to resist any attack. It is run out over the lines every two weeks, and requires about five days to make the circuit.

"Our payroll now is enormous, for we are pushing construction on several points of the road. It happened, this time, that two Denver banks wished to make gold shipments to the East. The recent railroad troubles have alarmed them, and they were anxious to secure absolute safety for their coin.

"Therefore they made special arrangements with us to have it carried on our train. We are responsible to a certain extent for its safety. But we felt absolutely no anxiety. Train robbers don't cut any figure with us. I tell you that a regiment of soldiers couldn't have taken that car without a cannon.

"We had a guard of twelve men, not counting the engineer and fireman, who were, of course, armed to the teeth. The guard consisted of picked fellows, every one of them worth a dozen ordinary men, for honesty, courage, and fighting qualities. The car was an arsenal. I impress these facts on your mind to show you that there is no question of an ordinary train robbery."

"I should say not," responded Nick, as the other paused and leaned his weary head on his hands. "In such cases it is not customary to steal the train. The contents satisfy the average train robber all right."

"What has become of it? Think of that. How can they have made away with that locomotive engine, and that iron-sheathed car? I'm nearly crazy about it, as you can see. Let me get back to my story:

"The train reached here all right at half-past seven o'clock on Monday night. The construction gang and the ordinary employees at this point were waiting for it, and were paid off. That required about three-quarters of an hour.

"From here, the train was to make a run to Monowai on the other side of the South Fork of the Republican River, arriving there about ten o'clock, and remaining at that point till daybreak. The train was reported at 8:25 at Freeze Out, ten miles east of here, where it stopped a few minutes, and then proceeded.

"The next signal station is Haskins, which is not a town, but merely a station from which a few cattle are shipped, once in a while.

"It passed that point without stopping, at 9:16, and nobody knows what became of it after that. It did not reach Monowai.

"It vanished off the face of the earth. It vanished with fourteen human beings and a million dollars of money."

Hampton got upon his feet as he said this, and his pale lips quivered with excitement.

"Be calm, Mr. Hampton," said Nick. "There's no use in taking this too hard, though I own that it's enough to upset anybody. You have examined the track beyond Haskins, of course."

"Mr. Carter, I have been over every foot of it. I can find no place where the train could have left the rails.

"And even if I had, what could have become of it afterward?

"It's an open stretch of country. There isn't a chance to conceal a baby carriage anywhere from Haskins to Monowai.

"But that doesn t cut any figure, for how could a locomotive be lifted bodily off the rails and carried away, if only for a few yards?"

"I don't know," responded Nick cheerily. "But I'm here to find out."

"What shall we do first?"

"I'll tell you what you'll do first," said Nick. "You'll go to bed."

Hampton arose and stretched himself.

"It's a fact that I'm nearly dead," he said. "I'll take some sleep, though only for a few hours. Hello, Barron!"

A tall, handsome young man came out of an inner room.

"My secretary and right-hand man," said Hampton. "Jim, this gentleman is Nick Carter, the celebrated detective. Tell him all you know."

Hampton staggered to a rude couch and fell upon it. He was asleep before he struck.

"If I tell you all I know," said Barron, frowning. "it won't help you much. This is positively the most infernally mysterious job on record. However, I have a theory about it which I will explain to you, if you'll come out along the road with me on an engine."

They found an engine just ready to pull a carload of laborers over to Monowai.

It wasn't a very high-toned special, but it went flying.

They shot through the town of Freeze Out like a cannon ball, and sped away toward Haskins, the last spot at which the pay train had been reported.

Seven miles beyond Haskins the road crosses the South Fork of the Republican River, which is a very peculiar stream at that point.

It runs through a gorge, and the bridge crosses it at a height of about a hundred feet above the water.

At this point Barron had the engineer stop, and he and Nick got out. The train then went on to Monowai.

The two men stood at the end of the bridge looking down into the stream.

"Do you know where I think that train is," said Barron.

Nick pointed down without speaking.

"Exactly," responded Barron. "I believe it's at the bottom of the river."

"Why don't you drag and find out?"

"Do you know how deep the water is there?"

"No."

"Neither does anybody else. The stream fills a sort of hole there and is fed below by springs. I believe the hole goes halfway down to China."

"Several hundred feet, I suppose."

"I don't know, but on my suggestion Hampton is going to find out."

"How do you suppose the train got down there? Not off the bridge, of course, or we'd see the marks."

"It ran off the bluff here."

"Then why isn't the track torn up and the top of the bluff scarred?"

"I'll tell you," said Barron. "I've studied on that point and at last I've made up my mind.

"This was no accident. That train was thrown into that place."

"Why?"

"Out of hatred for the men who are back of this railroad. They've got bitter enemies in these parts. If President Kane came out here, for instance, his life wouldn't be safe twenty-four hours."

"What's the matter?"

"It was a land deal. You understand how those things are worked. The railroad got a good deal the best of some people in the towns along here."

"Then this treasure was destroyed for the purpose of ruining or at least injuring the railroad corporation?"

"I believe it. But more than that, who can tell that the people who did it haven't a scheme for getting the special out of the bed of the river. Suppose, for instance, that they should send a diver down there with an electric light one of these dark nights."

"That looks plausible," said Nick. "Let's examine the edge of the bluff."

He scanned the ledge carefully.

"Something has happened here, sure enough," he said.

Barron looked triumphant.

"I told Hampton so," he cried. "The villains laid down a little piece of track with a switch and just threw the train off the bluff."

"It looks that way. Here are marks on the rocks as if something heavy had gone along. But the track must have led clear to the edge of the cliff. There are no scratches of wheels on the rock."

"Of course not. Do you suppose they wanted us to know where the train had gone?"

"Certainly not."

"I've kept dark about this thing, except to Hampton. I'd be afraid of my life to have it known that I'd got on to this secret."

"I shouldn't think it was much of a secret," said Nick. "This is the only place between Haskins and Monowai where the train could have gone."

"But some people don't see it."

"Then they must be blind. These marks on the rock are clear enough to be seen on a dark night."

"But Hampton doesn't take my view of them. He thinks it's absurd to suppose that robbers would throw the train into the water and destroy all the greenbacks that were aboard."

"Weren't they in a safe?"

"Yes, but the safe might have been open. The man in charge was probably counting out his money for the payments at Monowai."

"There's something in that."

"But Hampton is wrong. The train's down there. Now let's get away from here and walk down toward Haskins.

"Do you know, I don't think it's a good idea for me to be seen around this place too much. I believe that there are members of the gang on guard here in the caves and crevices of the banks, or in that scrub growth on the other side, and that they'd be glad to remove me if they suspected what I'd discovered. And they'd do you up in very short order if they knew who you were."

As if in answer to Barron's words two rifle-shots rang out from the opposite bank.

Barron fell flat on his face.

"Are you hit?" asked Nick, stooping beside him.

"No; and I don't want to be. That's what I'm down here for."

As Barron spoke the shooting was renewed.

A bullet cut through the rim of Nick's hat, and several others went uncomfortably close.

He, too, lay down, and thus availed himself of the shelter of the bank.

"It's no use trying to fight them," said the detective. "We can't see them, and it would take us an hour to get down where they are. As for finding them in that place, it's no job for any two men to tackle.

"However, we've drawn their fire, and that's one good thing. Hampton's men can drive them out, and keep guard here after this."

"They're mighty poor shots," grunted Barron, "or they'd have had us easily enough."

"I should think so."

The two men crept back from the bluff's edge.

As the place from which the shots had come was considerably lower than the place where they had stood, the bluff afforded them shelter as they crept away.

When they had reached a safe distance they arose and walked toward Haskins until overtaken by the engine which had drawn them over.

Nick got off at Freeze Out, after directing Barron to consult Hampton in regard to the watch at the bridge.

CHAPTER III

THE IDIOT

Freeze Out was a town that had had a "boom" and lost it. The mines had "petered out," and nothing was left of the once bustling town but the dregs of its vice.

It was a hard town. One really good mine in its vicinity kept it alive, and the owners and workmen in that mine furnished the only respectable element of Freeze Out's population.

Nick had no sooner got into the town than a crowd of men attracted his attention.

They seemed to be surrounding some person who was acting strangely.

Nick mingled with the crowd, and saw that the object of their attention was a queer-looking fellow, ragged and dirty, and apparently insane.

He seemed to be a young man, but his face had the hue of age.

There was a wound on his head which was clumsily bandaged with a great piece of cloth, faintly stained with blood in several places.

It was hard to tell what his clothes had been like when they were new, for they were absolutely in rags, and were covered with mud.

Nick made out, however, that they had been blue. In fact, they had something the appearance of a uniform.

The man's face was haggard beyond anything Nick had ever seen in a person not wasted by disease.

He looked as if he had been frightened half to death, and then starved to the very brink of the grave.

16

As Nick came up, the men who surrounded this strange object were asking all sorts of questions.

The man stared blankly at the surrounding group.

He seemed incapable of speech.

Sometimes he sighed and sometimes he laughed, but it was always with the strangest manner, as of a feeble-minded child.

Suddenly a voice rose above all the others.

It was a cry of wild excitement and surprise.

"Good God!" and the word was not an oath, but such an exclamation as one utters in the presence of a mystery which only the Creator can solve. "Men! Do you know who this is? It's Alvin Clark!"

Then there was such a scene of excitement as Nick had rarely witnessed.

In the midst of the tumult of voices the detective heard enough plain English to enable him to understand the situation.

This tattered wreck, this speechless idiot, was the sole survivor of the pay train's crew!

He had been one of the guards.

It is hard to imagine a stranger scene than that.

Here was a man who, after nearly four days, had come back as if from the grave.

Nobody in the group which surrounded him had believed that any of the fated crew of that train would return to the light of day.

Probably some of those present thought that the train was at the bottom of that strange chasm under the bridge over the North Fork. Others had wild, impossible theories as to its disappearance.

All thought the case to be the deepest mystery they had even known.

And this man, who must have seen all that had happened, had come back in a manner and in a condition of mind and body which only made the mystery deeper.

He seemed to understand nothing that was said to him; he showed no sign of recognizing any of those about him.

He stared blankly around him, and said nothing.

"We must take him home," said one of the men at last.

"What'll his mother do?" asked another.

He was a rough fellow, but the way in which he asked that question showed that he had a heart.

And the crowd was with him. A murmur of pity ran through it.

Nick was surprised to find that the mother of this young man lived in that place.

There were probably not twenty respectable women in Freeze Out.

"Somebody ought to go ahead and break the news to her," he suggested to a man beside him.

"That's right," was the response. "I'll do it. Bring him along slowly, and I'll run on ahead."

They led the tottering imbecile along.

He offered no resistance, and seemed not to know nor care where he was going.

They came at last to a little house, one of the neatest in all that region.

The sound of a woman's excited voice came to their ears as they approached.

Then a woman of fifty years, decently clad, and pretty even in her old age, ran out from the house.

The crowd divided. It was a fine sight to see the respect these rough men showed for her and her grief.

She ran straight to her son and threw her arms around his neck. Then for the first time he showed a trace of human intelligence, and found a voice.

"Mother!" he exclaimed, in a tone like a child's. "See how they've torn my clothes."

Then he began to cry.

"Who did it?" exclaimed half a dozen men together, carried away by their excitement.

But he would speak to nobody except his mother, and when she repeated the question he only said:

"I don't know. I'm awful hungry, mother, and I want a drink of water," and he followed her into the house.

"Is there a doctor in the place?" Nick asked.

"There's a doctor, but he's drunk all the time," was the response. "I'd rather trust Al Clark to his mother than to a hundred doctors like him."

Nick, on this description, was inclined to agree with the speaker. However, he felt that Clark should have medical attendance at once.

The detective is as good a physician and surgeon as can be found outside the very first rank of the profession, but he dared not make himself conspicuous by offering his services openly.

Instead he quietly passed the word around among the crowd that they ought to disperse, and the suggestion was accepted.

It was felt that nothing could be got out of Alvin Clark, and that the mystery of the pay train would have to wait for his recovery.

Such being the case, the men were naturally anxious to spread the news of his return throughout the town, and they went away to do it. So Nick was able to go to the door of Mrs. Clark's house unobserved.

She came in answer to his knock, and gladly accepted his services as a doctor. He frankly explained to her who he was and she promised secrecy. She led him to the bed on which her son lay, and then for the first time Nick had a chance thoroughly to examine the man's condition.

CHAPTER IV

ON THE BACK TRACK

Alvin Clark had many wounds, but none of them was dangerous in itself. He was bruised all over, as if he had been beaten, but upon close examination Nick decided that most if not all of these injuries were due to falling.

But there was a wound on his head which was of a different nature. It seemed to have been made by a bullet which had grazed the scalp.

He was suffering principally from the shock of so many injuries, and from the effects of some terrible experience which had prostrated his mind.

Whether he would ever recover his reason and be able to tell what had happened was a question which no human being could answer.

It was possible that a single night's rest would bring him to his senses, but it was far more probable that he would always remain what he then was, an idiot, without reason or memory.

Nick dressed his wounds and left him in the excellent care of his mother. Within a few minutes after leaving the house, Nick met Chick, who was disguised as a laborer on the railroad.

"I've learned nothing," said Chick. "The case is as blind as it can be."

"I agree with you, my lad."

"What do you think of Clark?"

"There's a faint hope that he may be able to clear up the mystery some day, but we can't wait for him."

"However, he must be carefully watched."

"Precisely. If any of the gang of robbers who did

this thing learn of his return, they may find it to their interest to put him out of the way."

"I'll look out for that."

"All right. That's the best plan. You guard that house."

While Nick sat on the station platform, an engine with a flat car came down the track from the direction of the river.

It stopped on Nick's signal, and the detective was surprised to find Hampton in the cab. Nick got in and the engine started.

"I'm feeling much better," said the railroad man. "I had a good sleep after you left, and I'm a new man for it. I've posted some men at the bridge. We couldn't find the fellows who shot at you."

They were then a mile from Haskins station in the direction of Freeze Out. Nick proposed that they stop the engine and begin investigation there.

"We have several matters to discuss privately," said the detective.

He then told Hampton of Clark's return.

"I can't understand it," said Hampton. "How could a man in such a condition have walked from the bridge to Stockton's ranch to say nothing of the mystery of his being alive after that plunge into the river."

"Nonsense, Mr. Hampton; he never took that plunge."

"What?"

"Nor the train either."

"Why, I thought that was settled now."

"I should say not. Now look here. I'm going to tell you something, and I want your solemn assurance that you won't tell anybody till I give you permission."

"You have my word on it."

"Well, that business at the bridge is too thin."

"What?"

"Mr. Hampton, if you stole a railroad train full of

money would you advertise the place where you had put it?"

"I should say not."

"Neither would anybody else. Well, that place is advertised."

"By the shooting?"

"No; by those marks on the rock."

"But they couldn't help that."

"Couldn't? I tell you the marks were made on purpose."

"What?"

"No train ever went off there. That's only a game. The robbers marked the rock with tools for the purpose of making you think the train was there."

Hampton struck one hand hard into the other.

"Mr. Carter," he cried, "you make me think better of my own head. Do you know I thought the same myself when I saw them."

"Good for you."

"Barron's a young man, and apt to let a theory run away with him, but I'm too old for that.

"I saw through that game, but I've kept still about it. Of course that shooting today was a part of the plot. I don't believe they really wanted to kill you. They were just lying low there for a chance to make a bluff."

"No; they were gunning for me all right. They knew I was a detective. Anybody might have guessed that, seeing me at work there on the cliff. They intended to kill two birds with one stone, and I was one of the birds."

"Then what do you make of the case altogether?"

"That train is somewhere else, of course."

"But where? There isn't another place between Haskins and Monowai."

"Why do you say between Haskins and Monowai?"

"Because the train passed Haskins and didn't pass Monowai."

"How do you know it passed Haskins?"

"The signal man reported it."

"Suppose he was mistaken about it. Wouldn't that be a great piece of luck for the robbers?"

"I should say so. It would put us on to the wrong section of the track and fool us completely."

"Don't you believe they thought of that beforehand?"

"Who?"

"The train-stealers. I certainly should if I'd been in their place."

"Well? What would you have done about it?"

"What would I have done? Why, just what they did."

"And what was that?"

"They bribed the man in that station."

Nick pointed ahead to where the light of the Haskins station could be dimly seen.

"Do you think they did that?"

"I feel reasonably sure of it. He is the man they would naturally select.

"In Monowai on one side, and Freeze Out on the other, the game could not be worked.

"There are too many people in those places. The failure of the train to pass would be noticed.

"But there is only one man who would know it here, and he's in the scheme."

"Then you think that the train never passed Haskins?"

"That's what I think."

"And that the trick was done between Haskins and Freeze Out?"

"No doubt of it."

Hampton spent several minutes in reflection.

"Look here, Mr. Carter," he said at last. "Do you believe that they could have worked their game as well in one spot as another?"

"What do you mean by that?"

"I mean the trick by which the train is made to disappear. Could they work that anywhere?"

"I don't know. I confess that the key of that puzzle is not in my hand at present, but I don't believe they could. I think they took advantage of some natural peculiarity."

"Like the river, for instance, into which we thought at first that the train had been thrown."

"Yes."

"But that is as likely to be on one side of Haskins as the other."

"Not a bit of it. If they had any help from nature they got it between Freeze Out and Haskins."

"Why do you say that?"

"Because, my dear fellow, if it had been between Haskins and Monowai, the man in that station would have been bribed to say that the train did not pass."

"That's good reasoning, Mr. Carter. You have convinced me that we must look for the scene of the crime between Freeze Out and Haskins."

"Which enables us to understand Clark's appearance in Freeze Out."

"Exactly. He might have walked ten miles to Stockton's, but not twenty."

"Right, Mr. Hampton; and, as you say, my reasoning is good. But I know something better, that I am trying to get, and that is—confession from the signal man."

CHAPTER V

THE SIGNAL MAN

The station agent at Haskins sat in the doorway of his cabin, which was also the telegraph office and the freight depot.

As has been said, this was not an important point on the road. It would not have been worth while to place a man there except that construction was going on along that section of the line, and it was convenient to store materials at Haskins.

This, of course, required a man to guard them.

John Hill had been given the berth. He was a tall young man, with a beard that grew all over his face and a bad pair of greenish gray eyes.

Considering the beard and the eyes, it might be said that Hill looked like a thief behind a hedge fence.

He had been a telegraph operator in the East; had strayed West and run his rapid course at Denver, after which he had taken the job at Haskins to keep him from starvation.

As he sat in the doorway that evening he noticed a man coming along the track from the direction of Freeze Out.

The man came along slowly, and appeared to be somewhat under the influence of liquor.

When at last he got within the lighted space before the door, he was seen to be ragged and rough-looking.

He stopped directly in front of Hill, and balanced himself on his legs with considerable difficulty.

Then for a minute he stared straight into the station agent's face.

Hill finally got nervous at this peculiar form of introduction, and with a volley of oaths he inquired:

"Who are you?"

"I'm a tramp," said the other with a hiccough.

"Well, you look it. I'll swear to that."

"But I ain't going to be a tramp much longer."

There was something so peculiarly insolent in the man's manner that Hill jumped to his feet in a rage.

"No," he yelled, "you ain't going to be a tramp much longer. You're going to be a corpse, unless you get out of here mighty quick."

"No; I shan't be a corpse, either," responded the other. "I'll be a man with money to spend."

The station agent laughed with a noisy, nervous cackle. Somehow he couldn't seem to get a start in this conversation.

He couldn't quite size up the other man, and he was aware that something was going to be sprung on him, though he couldn't guess what it was.

"Money to spend," he repeated. "Where'll you get it?"

"Out of you," responded the tramp, with a leer.

Hill couldn't understand why it was that he didn't shoot this man, or at least break his head, but for some reason the coolness of the ragged fellow was a puzzle that kept Hill guessing.

"Out of me?" he said, and laughed again. "You're crazy."

"Not much, Mr. John Hill. I've got a small load on, but I know what I'm about."

"I don't believe it."

"Then let me prove it to you," said the tramp. "I know what became of the pay train!"

Previous to this remark, Hill had sat down again in his rough wooden armchair.

When the tramp said those words, Hill gave such a start that he pulled one of the arms right off the chair.

"That seems to interest you," observed the tramp. "Here! Drop that gun!"

Hill had got a revolver half-drawn, but he was "covered" before he could use it. The tramp was much the quicker artist with a shooting-iron. The station agent dropped his weapon.

"Now we can talk it all over quietly," said the tramp, seating himself on the edge of the platform.

He still had his revolver ready, and Hill was at his mercy.

"What's your game?" asked the station agent, in a tone of desperation.

"This is it. I'm a tramp. I came through to Monowai from the East, and got kicked off a freight train there last Sunday night.

"I hung around till Monday night, and then started to tramp along toward Denver.

"It happened that I was sitting over there against that rock at just the hour when you reported that train as passing your station.

"It didn't pass, Mr. John Hill. Now, what do you think of that?"

"I think you're crazy," said Hill, but his voice betrayed him.

Nick Carter, playing the role of the tramp, knew that his game had won.

"It's no use denying it, Hill," he said. "I know what I'm talking about. You're in the deal."

"What do you mean?"

"You're bought by the gang that got away with that train. That's what I mean."

Hill muttered something which could not be understood. He was badly rattled.

"Take it easy," said Nick. "There's no harm done.

I won't make any trouble for you. I only want to be let in on the divvy."

As suddenly as a bent spring recoils, Hill leaped from his chair, and straight at Nick. Revolvers didn't cut any figure with him in such an emergency as that.

Nick might have killed the man, but he did not fire. He could not afford to risk losing a witness. He dropped his own revolver and met the man's wild rush with a straight left hand blow. It struck Hill on the chin and just stopped his headway.

For a single instant he was balanced accurately on his legs. The next, Nick sent in his right, and Hill dropped as limp as a rag. The detective gave a loud whistle, and Hampton appeared out of the surrounding darkness.

Nick, meanwhile, was bending over Hill and trying to bring him back to consciousness.

"It's all right," he said to Hampton, when the latter came up. "The man has been bribed sure enough. When he comes to I think we can get something out of him."

Hill revived in a couple of minutes. The first object his eyes rested on was the face of Hampton.

He instantly recognized the railroad superintendent, and knew that the worst had happened.

"You see how you're fixed," said Nick to him. "I'm a detective from the East, and you know Mr. Hampton."

Hill groaned.

"You're caught, my man, absolutely caught in a trap. The best thing for you is to make a clean breast of it."

Hill sat a moment thinking hard. Then he said:

"I deny everything. The train passed my station as reported. That's all I have to say."

Nick handed his revolver to Hampton.

"Keep a sharp eye on him," he said. "I'm going to make a hunt."

He went into the cabin. In five minutes he was back again holding a bag in his hand.

This bag gave forth a pleasant chink-chink when Nick knocked it against the side of the cabin.

"About five thousand in gold," said the detective. "I haven't had time to count it. I don't think they paid you very well, Mr. Hill."

Hill's face was ghastly.

"Now, my man," said Nick, "it's all over with you. Of course you know what kind of a job this was, or if you don't fully realize it, I'll tell you. It was a hanging job for every man in it. The murder of that train's crew will have to be avenged by the law."

"I don't believe they're murdered," said Hill. "But if they are, it was none of my doing."

"Come, come, speak up. Give us the whole story."

"What will you do for me if I will?"

"I make no promises now," responded Nick. "Let's hear what you have to say." Mr. Hampton, when appealed to, only said he would make it as light as he could for Hill.

"I'll take your word. Here are the facts: I was bribed to report that train as having passed my station, but not in the way you imagine. It was this way: Early that evening a man whom I had never seen before came in my cabin here, and got into conversation with me.

"Presently he pulled out a bottle of whisky and we began to drink. The next thing I remember, it was beginning to be light. What happened during the night I don't know, but of this I am sure it was that man and not I who sent the message reporting the train.

"When I woke up he was beside me with that bag in his hands. He said that the pay train had gone by, and that he had reported it because I was too drunk to do it. Of course I knew he was lying. I felt sure that the train had been held up, and I thought that it had probably been done right at this station.

"That was what I thought was his reason for drugging me. He made no denials when I accused him, but offered me this gold if I would keep still.

"He promised me as much more in two weeks' time, if I did not weaken meanwhile. That's all I know about the affair."

"You lie!" cried Hampton fiercely. "And you shall swing for this crime."

"Upon my word I believe that you will," said Nick calmly, "but I'll give you one more chance. If you'll tell me what became of that train, and give the names of the gang, I'll accept you as State's evidence at the trial, and allow you to go absolutely free.

"Come, there's an offer. You know me. Have you any doubt that I will do as I say?"

"No," said Hill in a husky voice, "but I can't do what you ask. I don't know what has become of the train. I don't know the name of a single member of the gang. I wish to heaven I did."

Hampton, beside himself with rage, stalked up to Hill with clinched fist.

Nick caught his arm.

"It's no use, Hampton," he said quietly. "This man is telling the truth."

CHAPTER VI

HOW MR. JOHN JONES PAID FOR THE DRINKS

Nick set about getting a description of the man from Hill and was told he was about Nick's size with a beard, undoubtedly a disguise. However, Hill was sure he would recognize him.

"You may have the chance," said Nick. "Now, Mr. Hampton, I suggest that you telegraph for an engine, and take this man quietly to Sumner where he can be kept under guard for a while.

"Then get a man about his height and weight whom you can absolutely trust, and send him to me.

"I'll fix him up to look like Hill, and we'll leave him at this station. Of course we mustn't let the gang know that Hill has been nabbed."

"Do you believe that the thieves are still in this region?"

"I believe that all or nearly all of them are in Freeze Out at this moment."

"That's my own idea, but I'd like to hear your reason?"

"You have had men out from the very first, quietly going about through this section. They haven't got a tip on anybody. No band of men has been seen. There are, in fact, no indications of the descent of any organized gang. But the work must have required a good many. I don't believe as many strangers could get in here without exciting suspicion somewhere.

"From this, I conclude that the scheme was organized right here in Freeze Out. Moreover, the exaggerated precautions which they have taken to conceal everything, show that they are anxious to gain a lot of time.

"That looks to me as if they were residents of the region and wanted a chance to get out quietly, one by one, without exciting suspicion. When we work down to this gang we'll find that it isn't composed of ordinary train robbers, but of careful men who want to spend the money they've stolen without being troubled by the fear of a sheriff at their elbows."

"I agree with you," said Hampton. He stepped to the telegraph and sent for an engine. It came in about an hour, and Hampton, with Hill, went to Sumner. Nick waited for daylight. Then the man, whom Hampton had promised to send, arrived. The detective disguised him so that he could pass for Hill.

Then Nick took a handcar which stood near the station and proceeded to survey the track between Haskins and Freeze Out once more. It was a down grade most of the way, and Nick let the car slide along while his eyes were busy with every detail of the country.

Again that dark mystery impressed itself upon him. How was it possible to conceal that enormous engine and the steelclad pay car so that no trace of it remained?

Nick held it for an absolute certainty that the train was somewhere in the ten miles of country between Haskins and Freeze Out, but he found no sign of it.

It was a queer country, mostly flat as the top of a table, but roughened here and there by hills which were merely great rocks thrust up through the surface by convulsions of nature in the remote ages of the past.

The track for several miles wound among these hills, some of which were bare and rugged, while others were covered with sand upon one side.

Nick viewed this unpromising country with the sharpest attention, but he saw absolutely nothing which helped to explain the strange thing that had happened.

When he ran the handcar upon a siding at Freeze Out he was no wiser than he had been when he started.

He went at once to have a talk with Chick, who was on guard in the vicinity of Mrs. Clark's house.

"There have been men hanging around this place to-night," said Chick, "but nothing has happened. If it was the intention to make away with Clark, I believe they have abandoned it.

"Anyway, the house is too well guarded now. Mrs. Clark's nephew came over from Sumner last night, and another relative got in from Denver this morning. They're both good men, and handy with a gun. Clark is safe while they stay."

"Then you can help me," said Nick. "We've got to get in with the men here. I believe that the gang is right in this town, and we must work down to it.

"We must adopt something extra good in the way of disguise. This is my idea: I'll be an Englishman, with more money than brains, and you'll be a Denver lawyer, supposed to be working the Englishman."

"Trying to sell him mining property, eh?"

"Yes. We'll arrive on the forenoon train from Denver. Ride up the track on an engine and board the train at the station beyond Sumner."

When that train arrived at Freeze Out the Englishman and the shark lawyer were aboard.

The mines around Freeze Out had proved to be, with a single exception, the rankest of failures. The people were desperate, and one or two games had already been put up to "salt" some of the mines, and sell them to suckers from the East.

Before the day was over Chick had succeeded in working into the confidence of one of the hardest characters in Freeze Out.

This was a man named Bob Willet, who looked exactly like old-fashioned pictures of the devil.

He had taken up several claims in the old days, and they had proven worthless. After that, he had made his living by poker and robbery.

Chick put up a game with Willet by which the Englishman was to buy Willet's claims. They were to be duly "salted," and then the trick was to be done. Chick knew that in case Willet had been in the train robbery, this game was a good one for him to play.

Selling a salted mine wouldn't get him into any trouble, but it would afford an excellent excuse for skipping the town, and would prevent anybody from thinking that Willet had skipped because of connection with the other affair.

The ease with which Willet went into his scheme convinced Chick that he had got hold of one of the men he was after. Willet was anxious to turn the trick as soon as possible, and he was not nearly so particular about the money part of it as he would have been in Chick's opinion, supposing that he had not already made his stake in another way.

However, this was only suspicion, and brought Chick little nearer to the solution of the mystery. Yet he worked Willet industriously while the Englishman was supposed to be sleeping off the effects of hard travel, at the miserable hotel.

It was about four o'clock in the afternoon when Nick, as the Englishman, came down from his room, and strolled into the bar of the hotel.

He paused just long enough behind a battered screen door to hear the bartender say:

"He's a good sucker for you, Jones. Why don't you sell him the Star and Garter?"

"Not me," said Jones. "I believe the mine's good yet, and I shall hold on to it."

A laugh greeted this remark.

"Gentlemen," said Jones, "the Star will show pay dirt yet." At this the Englishman entered.

The bartender winked at Jones. "You're right, Mr. Jones. It's a great piece of property."

"I beg pardon," said Nick. "Is it a mine? I'm interested in mines. I'd like to see it."

"I'll show it to you some day," said Jones curtly, and turned to leave the place.

The bartender chuckled, and muttered aside to one of the men who leaned against the bar: "He's playing him."

The man thus addressed said nothing, but he, too, began to walk toward the door.

"I say, Mr. Jones," called the bartender, "wasn't that last round of drinks on you?" Jones had already passed through the screen doors, and Nick after him.

The proud owner of the Star and Garter—which everybody knew to be a worthless hole in the ground—turned back and entered the barroom, leaving Nick outside.

"I believe it was on me," he said; and ran his hand down into his pocket.

At this moment Nick heard voices on the outside of the house. He heard Chick say:

"He seems to be out of his head."

And the next instant Willet responded.

"That's Alvin Clark. He's crazy."

Through the crack of the doors, Nick saw Clark enter the barroom. Just then Jones pulled his hand out of his pocket. He brought with it several coins, and one of them dropped on the floor. Instantly the imbecile leaped upon it, and seized it. Then he began to dance like a little child:

"It's mine! It's mine!" he cried.

Jones started back with a cry of astonishment.

Then, with a terrible oath, he drew his revolver.

But the Englishman was too quick for him. His hand was on Jones' arm, and the grip was like steel.

"Don't hurt the lad. He hasn't done any harm."

CHAPTER VII

A DEAD SURE CLEW

Jones put back his gun with a hollow laugh. He saw in an instant that he had made a mistake.

The town was rough enough, but it wouldn't have stood it if Jones had shot Clark. Jones would have been hanging to a tree within half an hour unless Nick could have saved him.

"I didn't mean to hurt him," he said. "You blasted Englishman, what a grip you've got. I believe you've broken my wrist."

"Beg pardon, I'm sure. I had no intention of hurting you. Let's have a brandy and soda all around, and forget this matter."

"The lad frightened me," said Jones. "I believe he's hoodooed."

While Nick and Jones were indulging in mutual apologies, and trying to convince each other that the incident amounted to nothing, Alvin Clark had been holding in his hand the coin which he had found on the floor. Jones noticed this.

"Here!" he cried, "give me back my money." He seized Clark by the wrist, and the idiot began to cry.

"It's mighty tough to see him like that," exclaimed one of the men, who had been included in Jones' unlucky treat. "A week ago there wasn't a smarter fellow than Alvin Clark between here and the Atlantic Ocean."

"'Pon my word," said Nick, "it's too bad to take the coin away from the poor beggar. I'll buy it of you, Mr. Jones, by Jove, and give it to him."

"No, no; let him keep it," said Jones. "Put it in your pocket, Alvin, and take it home."

"Let's see what it is, first," said Nick.

To everybody's surprise Clark handed him the coin.

"Why it's only an English ha'penny piece," said Nick.

Clark nodded his head and laughed foolishly. "And here's something on it," the detective continued. "Two letters, by Jove, an A and a C."

"Ha, ha, ha!" laughed the idiot. "I know. Didn't I say so? It's mine. A. C. That's me."

He danced up and down like a delighted child.

"He's right," cried the bartender. "That's his pocket-piece. I've seen him have it."

"Well, now, that's strange," said Nick.

"So it is," said the bartender. "How'd you come by it, Jones?"

"Blowed if I know," said Jones. "I don't believe I had it. I think he dropped it himself."

"That's it," exclaimed Willet. "He dropped it himself."

"What do you know about it, Bob Willet?" asked the bartender.

"I saw him through the door," replied Willet. "Just as Jones pulled his hand out of his pocket, Al Clark dropped that pocket-piece. It didn't come out of Jones' clothes. I'll swear to that."

The idiot seemed to hear not a word of what was said. He kept his eyes fixed on the coin which had passed back to Nick's keeping.

"Where did you lose this?" asked the detective.

Clark shook his head. He did not understand.

Nick still held the coin, and Clark began to cry.

"Give it back to me!" he said. "I want to show it to mother." The detective returned the coin. Clark darted out of the door.

"Will he have sense enough to go home?" asked one.

"Oh, yes," said Nick; "he's all right. He's the chap, I suppose, who was on that lost train? Well, he's not going to be a fool always. He'll come around all right."

All the men had moved toward the door, and were watching the idiot, who was walking up the long street which ran from the hotel in the direction of his mother's house. Nick, unperceived by any one, crept up behind his assistant.

"Get on to Jones and Willet," he whispered.

The two men stood just outside the door. They were muttering to each other.

"They're going to follow the lad and do him up if they can," said Nick. "That means that we've struck a dead sure clew at last. In my opinion that coin will solve the puzzle of this case.

"Follow Clark. Don't let him out of your sight, and remember what I said. He isn't always going to be a fool."

Chick turned and caught his chief's eye for a second. A flash of meaning was in that glance. A moment later Chick had passed out of the hotel, the other way, and was hurrying toward Mrs. Clark's house. Jones and Willett went off together.

"A very nice man, that Mr. Jones," said Nick. "I like a person who'll admit it when he's in the wrong."

The bartender laughed till the walls rang.

"Jones is a nice man, I don't think," he said. "Say, I'll bet you five that that man's done time in the States. Don't you have anything to do with him if you can help it."

"Why not?"

"Because he'll do you up. He's a dead sure man with a gun, and he doesn't like to have people grab him the way you did. So you look out or you'll get lead into you."

"Thank you; I'll take your advice," said Nick. He was glad to get these pointers on Mr. Jones' character, because they fitted in well with the other circumstances.

Meanwhile Chick was making his way to Clark's house.

He approached it from the rear. Alvin, who entered by the other way, passed straight through, apparently looking for his mother.

He did not find her, and at last he seated himself on the steps before the back door. Chick at once approached.

"Clark," he said, "do you know who I am?"

The idiot stared blankly.

"Well, I'm Chickering Carter, Nick Carter's assistant, and we're both out here on this robbery case. There are papers to prove what I say."

He threw down two or three documents beside Clark.

The idiot picked them up idly, and handled them without a sign of knowing what they were.

"Well, are you satisfied?" asked Chick.

Clark appeared to be playing with the papers. Then he suddenly threw them down, and called, "Mother!"

Nobody answered. Clark got upon his feet and went into the house. He was gone two or three minutes. Chick did not move. When Clark came back he resumed his seat on the steps, and looked up into Chick's face.

"Good," said the detective, "you've decided to trust me. You played it well; but you couldn't deceive Nick Carter's eye, nor mine either, for that matter.

"Yesterday it was genuine; today it's a fake. Yesterday you didn't know anything. You were an idiot, in fact, as well as in appearance. Today you know what you're about, and you're playing the part. I admire your skill, but I advise you not to waste it on your friends."

"I believe you're right," said Clark, in a calm and rational voice. "I have decided to tell you all that I know about this case."

CHAPTER VIII

A TRICK OF MEMORY

"I suppose you know all about the train," Clark began, "I mean what it carried, how it was guarded, etc."

"Yes; I've got all those facts."

"Then there's no use going back of the time when we left Freeze Out, that evening. It was already dark, and the night shut in blacker every minute. We ran rather slowly. I should say not more than twenty miles an hour. Two of the guards were on the front platform of the car, and two on the rear. The others were inside. I was one of the men on the inside.

"I didn't pay any attention to the time, and I can't say how long it was after we left Freeze Out, or how far we'd run when the thing happened. It is sure, however, that we were some distance this side of Haskins. All I know for certain is that we were just going around a curve.

"Suddenly there was the most awful sound. It seemed to me that the whole top of the car was ripped off. Then there was a dreadful shock, and the car turned up on one side. I felt myself flying through the air.

"It was no longer dark. There was a strange glare right in my face, and yet I couldn't see anything. I know that I struck the earth, and scrambled onto my feet. Then came a crash that seemed to split my head open.

"I remember nothing more until I found myself crawling on my hands and knees over rocks and through pools of water. It was perfectly dark, or else I was blind. There's a great question. I can't decide it.

"My recollection is confused. I remember that it seemed as if I had been crawling over those rocks for years and

40

years. I felt a thousand different agonies. I was bruised
and bleeding. My body from the shoulders to the knees
seemed to be entirely gone.

"I could not understand that peculiar sensation at first,
and then a thought came to me: This is hunger. I am
dying of starvation. I must have fainted, and revived
many times. It was like the delirium of fever.

"Sometimes I thought myself miles underground, and
again I seemed to be climbing over mountains. But always
I was creeping on my hands and knees amid utter darkness. Then there was a flash of light. I was dazzled.
This light struck straight into my face, and I felt parched
with the heat.

"I could not understand how the light had come to me
so suddenly, until, in a moment, I saw that it was the sun.
I had regained my sight. I was lying on the side of a
rocky hill in a place which I never had seen before.
Thirst consumed me. Hunger was entirely forgotten.

"With the greatest difficulty and pain, I got upon my
feet. I half-staggered, half-rolled down the side of the
hill. The remainder is a confusion of wild dreams. I was
in delirium. Sometimes I seemed to be flying through
the air. Again I was crawling as before.

"Sometimes I feasted upon everything that I ever liked
to eat, and I drank water that was cold as ice. Then
these things vanished and hunger and thirst returned.
At last I seemed to be surrounded by a thick cloud like
smoke. I could hear voices, but could not understand
what was said. At least one voice became clear, and as
I recognized its tones, the cloud seemed to grow thin in
the middle.

"I can't describe it except to say that it rolled away
on every side till it made a sort of round picture-frame.
And in the center was the picture. I'll tell you it was
that which I wanted most to see. It was my mother's
face. Slowly the objects about me grew clear. I was in

my room, in my own bed, and she was bending over me.

"That was this morning. For a long while I didn't dare to move. I was afraid that this was another vision like the dinners that had vanished just as I tried to eat, and the water which never quite wet my lips. But at last the reality impressed itself on my mind. My mother spoke to me. I answered her, and then I knew that I had come back to life.

"She told me to sleep, and very soon my eyes closed. When I awoke, I heard two other voices besides my mother's. Jack and Frank Austin were talking. They're my cousins, you know.

"I heard the whole story of the disappearance of the pay train, and then for the first time I realized a part of what had happened. They spoke about my coming home, and how I had lost my wits. They discussed their theories about the train. I made no motion. I was thinking it all over.

"Both of them believed that the train had been robbed and spirited away in some mysterious manner. I felt that that was true. They said that they believed that the gang of robbers was made up of men from Freeze Out who were still here.

"Then a plan came to me. I said to myself: 'The men who did that trick will be scared by my return. They will be afraid that my memory will come back to me. It's a sure thing that they will try to put me out of the way. If I pretend to be still out of my head they'll regard it as an easy job. And I'll get the drop on the first man who tries it!'

"That looked pretty good, didn't it? Well, I resolved to try it. I knew that my mother wouldn't let me get out of the house if she knew about it, so I waited till Jack and Frank had persuaded her to go and lie down. She'd been watching by me all night, and hadn't slept much, in fact, since I disappeared.

"When she had gone Jack went out, leaving Frank to watch. I told him my game, and persuaded him to let me try it. So I got out of the house, and went to the hotel barroom, where I knew that I'd find the toughest crowd, and the men most likely to have been in that game.

"You saw the result. When that coyote, Jones, attempted to pull that gun on me, he convicted himself.

"And then the coin! There was great luck. I always said that that was my lucky piece."

"Then that was a genuine thing? Jones really dropped it."

"Sure."

"Well, that settles it, so far as he is concerned."

"Yes; and it fixes that man, Willet, too."

"No doubt of it. His eagerness to support Jones' story lets him in all right."

"So we have two of the gang spotted already."

"We have."

"And you can take them at any time."

"I can, but I won't."

"You won't?"

"Well, I guess not."

"Why?"

"What good would that do?"

"Make them squeal."

"What, those two men! Not much. You ought to know them better than I do, Clark, but you don't seem to."

"Perhaps you're right."

"Of course I am. They'd give me the laugh."

"But how about that half-penny?"

"That's good enough evidence for us, but I don't think we'll go into court on that alone. There are several other things that we need."

"It's a good starter, though."

"First rate; but the main question is just where it was before. What's become of that train?"

"I give it up."

"Can't you remember any more of what happened at the time when the train left the rails."

"No; I've tried and tried, but that's all I can recall. There's one point, though."

"What's that?"

"You say 'when the train left the rails.' Now the queer part of it is that the train didn't seem to leave the rails at all."

"You don't mean it."

"It's a fact. I've tried to puzzle it out, and I'm certain of this much: the train ran absolutely smooth up to the moment when that shock came.

"I'm a railroad man, and I know how it feels when a train goes off the track. It didn't feel that way.

"It was more like a collision."

Chick thought a moment. Then he said:

"Did you feel the brakes just before that shock?"

"It seems to me that I did, but only for a half-second."

"However, that shows that the engineer saw something ahead."

"Yes; there's a point, but here's another: He must have been right on top of it before he saw it."

"You say that you were going round a curve?"

"Yes."

"That may explain it in part. And it gives us a clew. Wait. we'll get another. Which way was the train turning on that curve?"

"To the right. I felt the lift of the other side of the car."

"Good. Now we should be able to locate the spot."

"I should think so. We shall have only four or five miles of track to examine, for we were several miles out of Freeze Out when it happened, and the track is straight for quite a distance this side of Haskins."

"Right. I've looked it over carefully."

"Have you formed an opinion yet as to this case?"

"No; I haven't."

"Could they have dug a big pit alongside the track and switched us into it?"

"Did you feel the fall?"

"No; I didn't. I'm sure we weren't dumped that way, and yet I can't think of anything else.

"But it wasn't that. The first thing that hit us struck the car roof. The shock wasn't on the bottom. It was on top."

"Well, we won't waste time in speculation," said Chick. "I'm going out along that track."

"I'll go with you."

"No, you won't. You'll go to bed. You're not strong enough yet for any such job."

Clark protested, but the argument wound up by Chick's putting him to bed, and posting both the Austins as guards over him. Then Chick went out and found Hampton, the superintendent. To him Chick outlined the results of his talk with Clark.

Then the two men quietly got on an engine, and started off along the track. For several miles they rode in silence.

"There are three curves that answer all the conditions," said Hampton, at last. "And here's one of them."

The track at that point bent sharply to the right to avoid the end of a long hill or ridge of rock, rising from a sweep of sand, which rose in a tall bank against the end of the hill. The engine was stopped, and Chick began to circle the base of this hill.

"Hello!" he cried presently. "There's a coyote. I haven't seen one in many a day."

"Wonder what he's after?" said Hampton.

The hideous brute was digging in the sand about a

hundred yards away from the track. Chick walked toward the coyote, which fled.

"He's made quite a hole here," said Chick. "Suppose we see what he was after."

Hampton ridiculed the idea as a waste of time, but Chick got a fireman's shovel from the engine, and proceeded to dig. In five minutes he had uncovered a man's arm.

He seized it, and dragged the body into view. It was that of a man of middle age, dressed in a blouse and overalls. There was a bullet wound almost exactly in the middle of his forehead. Hampton uttered a cry of horror at the sight of him.

"It's Joe Anthony," he exclaimed. "The engineer of the pay train!"

The engineer and fireman ran up, and they, too, identified the body. They were wildly excited, and breathed vengeance upon the authors of this murder. Hampton was even more moved, and Chick's demeanor was by no means so calm as usual.

The four men, with such tools as they could muster, threw up the sand in every spot where there was the slightest indication that it had been previously disturbed.

Their search was unrewarded. The engineer's body was the sole relic of the great and marvelous crime.

No trace of the other men who must have perished with him, nor any fragment of his engine or of the gold-weighted car which it had drawn, could be found.

CHAPTER IX

THE DANGER SIGNAL

Nick, meanwhile, had kept his eyes on Jones and Willet. They had taken the affair in the barroom very seriously.

However, they did nothing during the afternoon, and shortly before six o'clock they separated, each going in the direction of his home. Nick could not follow both of them, and he had to make a choice. He selected Jones, for the coin had implicated him in the crime.

Jones lived on the edge of the town, and occupied a very decent house, as houses go, in Freeze Out. He lived alone, except for an old Indian woman who cooked for him, and kept an eye on the house. As she had the reputation of shooting as well with a rifle as any man could, Jones' property was never molested in his absence.

Nick followed his man home, and lay concealed in sight of the house. He could look in through the kitchen window, and he saw Jones stow away an ample supper. As it began to grow dark, Willet arrived. This suited the detective exactly. He did not want either of these men to be out of his sight longer than was absolutely necessary.

Nick had a theory of what was likely to happen.

It seemed certain that Jones and Willet were members of a gang which had organized the robbery.

They had been alarmed by the return of Clark, and especially by the incident of the coin. They would doubtless wish to communicate with the rest of the gang in order to form some plan of action.

The chances were that a meeting of the robbers would be held that night. It seemed incredible that the robbers would dare to remain in town after Clark's return unless they had reason to be perfectly certain that he did not know any of them.

They would probably make a plan for a speedy exit from Freeze Out. The gang would scatter, of course, each man taking his share of the plunder with him.

If that move should be successfully executed it would be next to impossible to capture all the guilty persons, or to recover all the stolen money.

The only way to handle the case was to catch the gang together and make a grand round-up of the villains. No more favorable opportunity could occur than the meeting of the gang, which Nick had reason to believe would occur that night. It would be necessary to find out where that meeting was to be held, and then to descend upon it with a sufficient force. After Willet had gone into the house Nick crept under the kitchen window.

It had to be cleverly done, for one of the men was on the watch all the time. But Nick has no superiors in this line of "stalking," and he succeeded in working his way along the side of the house till he lay under that window unperceived by Willet, who was looking out straight over the detective's head.

"I've got enough of this," he heard Jones say. "We're taking too big chances."

"I'm feeling the same way," responded Willet, "and yet if Al Clark could be got out of the way tonight I should feel fairly safe."

"How are we going to do it? The Austins are on guard, and just as soon as a racket is raised the whole town will be on top of us. I tell you that it's no use."

"It beats me to understand how he got away."

"And me, too. Why, the man was dead. I could have sworn to it. There he lay, as I supposed, with the whole top of his head blown off."

"And gold all around him, eh?"

"What's that got to do with it?"

"Nothing, my son, except that if you hadn't got away with some of the stuff, in violation of our agreement, you wouldn't have picked up that coin which had dropped from his pocket, and it wouldn't have dropped out of yours afterward."

"Curse it! Was there ever such infernal luck!"

"It should teach you to be on the square. You had no business to be swiping any of the stuff."

"Well, we won't fight about it. You're not going to give me away, Willet. A box of specie had burst, and while I was gathering it up, I just naturally stuffed a little into my clothes. I guess all the boys did the same."

"I didn't. The pile is all there so far as I'm concerned."

"Well, it's got to be got out of there, and quick, too. It may be found."

"Nonsense. Hampton thinks that the train went over the bridge. That game has worked to perfection. We're safe as a church except for that man Clark, and he's got to be done up. Then we can carry out the original plan. We'll start a rumor of a big strike of ore in the San Marco region. Half this town will take the trail next morning, as you know, for there's nothing to keep anybody here.

"We go out with the others, only instead of being on a hunt for gold we take our gold with us. Who'll be the wiser. Nobody will think anything of our getting out. We won't come back. Neither will half the others who strike out for the San Marco.

"Each of us goes where he wants to, and lives like a lord all the rest of his life. There'll be no reward offered for him; no trouble of any kind. That's the way to do a job of this sort and be easy in your mind afterward."

"Well, it looks good, but we can't lose time."

"Let's call the gang together, and come to a decision tonight. We'll give them the danger signal, of course."

"Well then, here goes. Take that, and fix your signals."

Nick heard a peculiar ripping sound. He couldn't make out just what it was, but he was extremely anxious to know. These men were preparing a signal to their comrades in crime. He must learn what it was in order to recognize it afterward.

Willet had stepped away from the window for a moment. Nick raised his head cautiously. He was taking his life in his hands, and he knew it, for a shower of lead would certainly follow detection. In spite of the danger he determined to see the inside of that room.

In a second his eyes were above the level of the window-sill. There was a table in the middle of the room, with a lamp on it. Jones had something in his hands which looked like a shirt. But Nick had no time to see clearly, for at that instant, Willet, who was standing on the other side of the table, perceived Nick. Willet's head was almost over the lamp. He blew straight down the chimney, and the room was dark. At the same moment he whipped out a revolver, and fired point-blank at Nick.

The bullet went so near to the top of Nick's head that he actually felt it. He had not ducked an instant too soon.

The game was up, at that point. Nick had no desire to engage in a shooting match, however good his chances might be of coming out best man. These two rascals were too valuable to him. He could not afford to shoot either of them. Instead, he took to his heels. Jones and Willet came after him, shooting as they ran.

He had made such a good start that neither of his pursuers was able to get out of the house in time to clap an eye on him. They simply shot on general direction, taking all the chances.

Nick did not run far. He dropped in some bushes, and, a second later, the two men rushed by in pursuit of him. Then the detective got up and ran after them. It took them only a few minutes to make up their minds that they could not overhaul their man.

They did not return to Jones' house, but kept on toward the center of the village. Presently they separated. Nick followed Jones.

He went to the hotel barroom, which was full of men. Nick, as the Englishman—a disguise which he had not used in his adventure at Jones' house—dropped in as if he had come down from his room in the hotel.

The detective kept a sharp eye on Jones. That worthy was up to something but he managed it very cleverly. It took diligent watching on Nick's part to discover that Jones, as he went about through the crowd, slipped something into the hands of some of the men.

Nick could not see what it was, but he saw one or two of the men who received it change color and draw in their breath suddenly, as if startled.

The detective spotted half a dozen of them. He noticed that they quietly slipped out of the barroom soon after receiving that which Jones had brought to them. When he had made up his mind as to the nature of this game, Nick followed one of the men out into the street. The fellow hurried along, but Nick kept near him.

Suddenly, in a particularly dark place, the detective sprang upon his victim. It was all over in half a second. The man found himself on the ground with an iron hand compressing his windpipe.

He was bound and gagged in short order, and then Nick dragged him to the loneliest spot which he could find without wasting too much time about it.

Nick was sorry that he could not put this man in a safer place, but there was no help for it. It was necessary to get after another member of the gang without delay, in order to track him to the meeting-place. Nick intended to go there disguised as the man whom he had captured.

With this end in view, he had removed the prisoner's coat and hat, and made a study of his appearance, which was sufficient for such a consummate master of impersonation as Nick Carter.

In the pocket of the coat Nick found the thing which had been passed to this man by Jones. It was a little strip of red flannel. This was, of course, the danger signal mentioned in the conversation which Nick had overheard.

On one side had been marked with charcoal the number eleven. Without doubt that meant the hour of the meeting. The detective hurried back to the hotel. Jones was still in the barroom. Nick resolved that he would track Jones when the latter left to go to the place of meeting.

Meanwhile he was anxious to find somebody whom he could send with a message to Hampton. It would be necessary to get together a force of trusty men in a hurry, for the robbers were not going to surrender without a struggle. A first-class scrimmage might be confidently expected when they should be surrounded and brought to bay.

Nick had had some hope of finding Chick there. He was, of course, unaware of the circumstances which had detained his assistant.

Time was pressing, and the detective had nearly decided to trust his judgment in the selection of a messenger, when James Barron, Hampton's secretary, appeared on the scene.

Nick made a sign to him, and then stepped outside. Barron followed as soon as he prudently could do so.

They stood near enough to the door to keep a lookout for Jones.

"Where's Mr. Hampton?" asked Nick.

"Gone off along the track with your friend. What's up?"

"I'm going to corral this gang of ruffians tonight, and I need a posse."

"I'll get word to the sheriff."

"It would be better to get Hampton. I'd rather have him at the head of the men. We need twenty at least."

"I can get them."

"Do it, and be mighty careful. Don't speak to anybody that you're not sure of."

"I'll look out for that."

"If you can possibly connect with Hampton, let him pick the men, and come at the head of them."

"How will he know where to go?"

Nick took a handful of small objects like cartridges out of his pocket.

"These things," he said, "are red lights. The fuses burn half an hour, and then the light flashes up.

"The flame is very bright. Such a night as this you could see it a mile away. As soon as Willet starts off and I get his general direction I'll set one of these lights.

"A quarter of a mile farther on I'll set another. The meeting is set for eleven o'clock.

"I don't think Jones will start inside of an hour. So you have that much time to collect your men.

"Then follow the lights, and don't let anything hold you back, for my life will depend on you."

"Depend upon me."

"As soon as you have half a dozen men together go and get a prisoner whom I have taken." He described the man and the place where he had left him.

"All right," said Barron; "I'll attend to him."

"Now you're off. Be quick and careful."

Barron nodded, and disappeared in the darkness.

CHAPTER X

Nick waited more than an hour for Jones.

In the course of that time, most of which he spent in the barroom, he saw the danger signal passed to three more men. Thus he had already spotted nearly a dozen members of the gang.

They were a desperate crowd, and, to judge by their faces, not lacking in either courage or cunning.

"We shall have a hard time with these fellows," said Nick to himself.

A little before ten o'clock Jones started off. His fellow-conspirators had left before him.

As soon as he could get outside the barroom, Nick secured the coat and hat which he had left in a convenient place, and he immediately assumed the appearance of the man whom he had made prisoner.

Jones started off in the direction of his house, but quickly turned aside, and keeping out of sight of the men who were lounging about the streets, he struck out for the open country.

On the outskirts of the town Nick placed his first signal fire. From that point on, he set them every five hundred yards.

The first of them had flamed up and Nick had seen its faint glow far behind him, and still Jones kept straight on across the open country in the direction of the rocky hills already described.

The rascal was late at the appointed place for it was half-past eleven when he stopped before the mouth of a tunnel in the hillside. From description Nick recognized this as the opening of the Star and Garter mine, in which

Jones had sunk many thousands of dollars of his own and other people's money.

After a glance behind him (which gave, however, no glimpse of the wily detective so close upon his heels) Jones plunged into the gloomy mouth of the tunnel.

Nick followed him after setting two of his signals above the opening. The tunnel, which began halfway up the hill, soon branched to the right, following the direction of the ridge. It bent slightly downward. The way was fairly clear, and Nick followed without difficulty the flickering light of the candle stuck in the front of Jones' hat.

They walked for nearly a thousand yards underground when suddenly a stern voice halted Jones.

He gave a sort of password, and was recognized. Nick was near enough to catch the words.

A minute later, when he himself was hailed, he called back the answer "pay dirt" without hesitation, and was allowed to pass, for his disguise deceived the sentry. A hundred steps brought him to a place where the tunnel was much enlarged.

It was, in fact, a chamber in the rock, partly natural, and partly the work of men. Three great torches lighted it, and threw their glare into the faces of the band of brigands, who were ranged along one of the walls.

There they all were—the men whom Nick had seen receive the danger signal, and others, making the total number up to fifteen.

But it was not upon these men that Nick bent his gaze. The other side of the cavern was more interesting.

For there lay the pay train, its great engine crushed and twisted; its strong car roofless and overturned!

How this miracle had been accomplished was, for some minutes, a mystery to the detective.

Then he recalled the course which he had taken in his subterranean walk.

Starting more than half a mile from the railroad track, he had followed the tunnel back until he knew that he must now be very close to the line of the iron highway.

Beyond the ruins of the train, he could see a continuation of the tunnel, but it appeared to end in a rude framework of boards and timbers. A great quantity of sand had sifted down through the boards.

By this, and by the appearance of the low arch of rock just beyond the wreck, Nick knew that this tunnel extended beyond the ledge, and a little way into the sand which some strange trick of nature had piled against the hillside. Therefore, only that board structure, and a thin layer of sand separated them at that moment from the outer air.

Beside the locomotive, but not a part of the wreck, were numerous sections of what seemed to be a sort of bridge made of timber and iron, and bearing rails nailed as on a railroad track.

From a view of these objects, the whole plan of the conspirators became clear to Nick.

A tunnel of the Star and Garter mine extended near to the edge of one of those queer hills which bordered the railroad track.

The conspirators, headed doubtless by Jones, the principal owner of the worthless mine, had extended the tunnel until it ran out into the sand bank, which was prevented from caving in by a cleverly built structure of timbers and planks.

Then they had built that sectional bridge, which could be quickly and easily fitted together, forming a section of track about a hundred feet long, and strong enough to bear a locomotive or at least to guide its course.

On the night of the disappearance of the pay train, they had laid this track from the main line to the mouth of the tunnel, from which the sand had been cleared away.

A switch had been quickly set, and when the pay train came booming along it had been thrown onto the false track, and straight into the tunnel, where it had been dashed almost to splinters by the rocky walls of the cave.

Scarcely any of the guards could have escaped death in the shock of this tremendous collision. The condition of the engine and car was proof of that to Nick.

In passing under the low roof of the tunnel the car's top had been torn off, and then it had been almost split in two by the tender ahead of it, after which it had toppled over in ruins. To dispatch the wounded and dying guards must have been an easy matter.

Then all that was necessary was to take up the moveable section of track with the switch; to replace the rails on the main track which had been cut to put in the switch, and finally to start a small sand-slide from the hill which in half a minute would effectually cover the mouth of the tunnel, and destroy all traces of the train's passage.

As the sand was always sliding down those hills, no change in the surface would be noticed, especially as, by the robbers' trick at the bridge, attention was directed to another part of the line.

This explanation of what he saw passed swiftly through Nick's mind. It had been a clever plot and well executed. A great deal of hard work had been done, but the reward was ample.

It lay before the robbers at that moment in the form of many boxes of gold coin and packages of greenbacks.

Nick was recalled to a consideration of his next move by the voice of one of the robbers addressing him.

"You're late, Jack Harding," he said. "Did you wait for Jones?"

"No; I came along as soon as I could," responded Nick, copying the voice of the man he was personating.

"There's another fellow later than you are," said another of the conspirators.

"Who's that?"

"Why, Jim Barron, our friend on the inside."

"He's here now," broke in another voice.

"Yes, I'm here," said Barron, striding into the cave with Jack Harding, the man whom Nick had made prisoner, at his side.

CHAPTER XI

"COME ONE—COME ALL"

In all his experience Nick had never been in so tight a place. The situation seemed utterly hopeless.

He was caged in that underground room, from which escape was impossible. It could hardly fail to be his tomb. But Nick never gives up without a struggle.

Though taken all aback by the sudden discovery that Barron was one of that murderous band, he did not for a second lose his marvelous self-control.

If he could have reached the tunnel he might have made a dash for safety, but almost the whole party stood between him and that passage. To gain it was impossible. What remained? Only to sell his life as dearly as possible.

The sudden discovery that there were two Jack Hardings present left the villains in momentary doubt which was the genuine, and profiting by this hesitation, Nick leaped backward beyond the wreck of the pay train.

A portion of its iron top which had been knocked off by the low roof of rock, lay just where it would best serve Nick for a shield. He leaped behind it, and in an instant his revolvers rang out.

Even if Nick had not been the prince of pistol-shots it would have been impossible for him to miss a man in such circumstances. They were too well bunched.

As it was, more than one bullet laid low a second victim after piercing the first, and the conspirators were thrown into confusion. They shot wildly and at random.

A few bullets struck Nick's shield, but he was unharmed, while his enemies were falling fast.

But among them Jim Barron seemed to bear a charmed life. Whenever Nick shot at him somebody stepped in front and received the bullet. And through all the tumult of the shooting, Barron's voice rang out.

"Go it, boys!" he yelled. "The more dead men, the more money for the rest of us. Mow 'em down, Nick Carter, while your lead holds out!"

Ah, that was the point. Nick had only two cartridges in his six-shooters when Barron uttered these words. He was doomed, and he felt it, but he resolved that Barron, the traitor, should "go over the divide" first. The detective ceased firing.

"Now we've got him, boys!" yelled Barron. "His ammunition's gone." He rushed forward with the others.

Nick's right-hand weapon flashed, and Barron reeled back, shot through the heart. Another dead villain. Then Nick hurled his empty pistols in the faces of his advancing foes, prostrating two more of them, and drew his knife for the final struggle which must be without hope.

They closed upon him without firing. Those in the front rank had emptied their revolvers, and the others could not shoot without hitting their friends. And in the comparative quiet which succeeded this fusillade, arose a strange sound. It came from behind Nick—a rushing, grinding sound accompanied by a muffled outcry of many voices. Then the board partition fell in, and through a deluge of sand a man sprang forward and took his place by Nick's side.

"Come on, you devils!" he yelled. "Come one, come all!"

And he sent a shower of bullets into the faces of the ruffians, who stood like statues, paralyzed by the sudden and miraculous nature of this interruption.

It was Chick. Hampton and a large force of men poured in after him. The ruffians broke and fled; as many of them as had not fallen.

"It's all right," said Chick to Nick, "let them go. The mouth of the cave is guarded."

"Chick," said Nick, grasping his friend's hand, "how did this most fortunate thing happen?"

Chick related the incident of the finding of the engineer's body.

"I reasoned it out from that," he said. "And then I sent for this force to dig in here and make a sure thing. Of course I knew that the other opening would be guarded.

"I had learned from Mr. Hampton about the Star and Garter mine. He did not know, however, that the tunnel came anything like so near to this side of the hill. Why, it's less than a hundred feet in a straight line from the spot where we stand to the track.

"They had to lay only a little more track than that, for the curve of the line made it unnecessary for them to waste any effort on a curve to meet the rails.

"A dozen of them could have laid that sectional track, and put in the switch in an hour and a half easily, considering that they had every measurement taken, and every spike all ready to go into its place.

"The engineer must have jumped when he saw the mouth of the tunnel, and have been killed outside by some of the gang. We shall find the bodies of the others hereabouts."

Hampton, meanwhile, had been examining the piles of treasure.

"Very little is missing, so far as I can see," he said.

"Our loss in money will be small, but I am sick at heart when I think of the brave fellows who lost their lives by this brutal plot of robbery."

"They have been amply avenged," said Chick, looking around upon the dead robbers. "You must have done some great shooting, Nick."

An exploration of the cave revealed the burial place of the murdered guards and of the fireman of the train. They had been dragged away into a branch tunnel, and piled there like so much timber. Their removal, as may be imagined, was a terrible task.

"There's one point that I don't understand," said Hampton, as they stood at the mouth of the Star and Garter mine while the prisoners were being led away through the gray mists of early morning.

"What is that?" asked Nick.

"How Al Clark escaped."

"I solved it," said Nick. "From the far side of the place where the bodies were piled is a low passage which leads into another tunnel. The murderers probably supposed that it was closed. Or perhaps they didn't care.

"At any rate, Clark must have revived after being laid with his dead comrades, and have made his escape by means of another entrance to the mine. The one by which I came in was, of course, guarded."

But little more remains to tell. In spite of Nick's best efforts, Judge Lynch got the prisoners who were taken on that night. The signal man Hill, not really a member of the gang, escaped with a ten years' sentence. So the entire gang was wiped off the face of the earth.

POPULAR CULTURE IN AMERICA

1800-1925

An Arno Press Collection

Alger, Jr., Horatio. **Making His Way;** Or Frank Courtney's Struggle Upward. n. d.

Bellew, Frank. **The Art of Amusing:** Being a Collection of Graceful Arts, Merry Games, Odd Tricks, Curious Puzzles, and New Charades. 1866

Browne, W[illiam] Hardcastle. **Witty Sayings By Witty People.** 1878

Buel, J[ames] W[illiam]. **The Magic City:** A Massive Portfolio of Original Photographic Views of the Great World's Fair and Its Treasures of Art . . . 1894

Buntline, Ned [E. Z. C. Judson]. **Buffalo Bill;** And His Adventures in the West. 1886

Camp, Walter. **American Football.** 1891

Captivity Tales. 1974

Carter, Nicholas [John R. Coryell]. **The Stolen Pay Train.** n. d.

Cheever, George B. **The American Common-Place Book of Poetry,** With Occasional Notes. 1831

Sketches and Eccentricities of Colonel David Crockett, of West Tennessee. 1833

Evans, [Wilson], Augusta J[ane]. **St. Elmo:** A Novel. 1867

Finley, Martha. **Elsie Dinsmore.** 1896

Fitzhugh, Percy Keese. **Roy Blakeley On the Mohawk Trail.** 1925

Forester, Frank [Henry William Herbert]. **The Complete Manual For Young Sportsmen.** 1866

Frost, John. **The American Speaker:** Containing Numerous Rules, Observations, and Exercises, on Pronunciation, Pauses, Inflections, Accent and Emphasis . . . 1845

Gauvreau, Emile. **My Last Million Readers.** 1941

Haldeman-Julius, E[manuel].**The First Hundred Million.** 1928

Johnson, Helen Kendrick. **Our Familiar Songs and Those Who Made Them.** 1909

Little Blue Books. 1974

McAlpine, Frank. **Popular Poetic Pearls,** and Biographies of Poets. 1885

McGraw, John J. **My Thirty Years in Baseball.** 1923

Old Sleuth [Harlan Halsey]. **Flyaway Ned; Or, The Old** Detective's Pupil. A Narrative of Singular Detective Adventures. 1895

Pinkerton, William A[llan]. **Train Robberies, Train Robbers, and the "Holdup" Men.** 1907

Ridpath, John Clark. **History of the United States,** Prepared Especially for Schools. Grammar School Edition, 1876

The Tribune Almanac and Political Register for 1876. 1876

Webster, Noah. **An American Selection of Lessons in Reading and Speaking.** Fifth Edition, 1789

Whiteman, Paul and Mary Margaret McBride. **Jazz.** 1926